Freeman

OLWEN

Text © Elena Morus/Siân Lewis 1997

*All rights reserved. No part of this publication
may be reproduced or transmitted, in any form
or by any means, without permission.*

*Published with the aid
of the Arts Council of Wales.*

ISBN: 0-86381-393-3

Design: Alan Jones

Illustrations: Carys Owen

*First published in 1996 by Gwasg Carreg Gwalch,
Iard yr Orsaf, Llanrwst, Wales LL26 0EH.*

☎ 01492 642031

Printed and published in Wales

STORIES FROM WALES

Olwen

Elena Morus
Adapted by Siân Lewis

GWASG Carreg Gwalch

Culhwch was a brave young knight. One day, when he was riding, he saw a girl with flowing golden hair.

Her skin was white as sea foam.

Her cheeks were red as roses.

Wherever she walked, four white clover grew beneath her feet.

Her name was Olwen and she was beautiful.

Culhwch fell head over heels in love with Olwen. He couldn't help it.

'Olwen,' he said. 'Will you marry me?'

But Olwen replied sadly, 'My father, Ysbaddaden, King of Giants, will not let me. On the day I marry he will die.'

Culhwch went to Ysbaddaden's castle.

'What do you want, you worm?' the giant roared.

'I am Culhwch,' the young man replied, 'and I have come to ask if I may marry Olwen.'

'Marry Olwen?' said the giant. 'Let me have a look at you.'

His servants pushed up his heavy eyelids with long forked poles.

'Well, Culhwch,' Ysbaddaden said. 'Come back tomorrow and you shall have your answer.'

Next day, when Culhwch returned, the giant was waiting.

'I have a list of tasks for you,' he said. 'You'll have to do them all, if you want to marry Olwen.

First fetch me the blood of the Black Witch to soften my beard. Then find the sword of Wrnach the giant.

Pluck the comb and scissors from the head of the great boar, Twrch Trwyth.

Gather the flax seeds from my field one by one.'

The list went on and on and on. When he came to the end, the giant laughed.

'You little shrimp,' he said to Culhwch. 'You'll never find all these things.'

'I will,' said Culhwch and left at once for the court of his cousin, King Arthur.

King Arthur gathered all his cleverest knights around him — Cai, Bedwyr, Gwythyr, Gwion Cat's-eyes, Gwrhyr who understood every language in the world, Clust who could hear the sound of an ant fifty miles away, Drem who could see a tiny fly rise in the air as far away as Scotland and Sgilti Lightfoot who walked so softly that not a blade of grass would bend beneath his feet.

'Culhwch,' said Arthur. 'I promise we'll never leave you till you have married Olwen.'

So the knights travelled far and wide to find all the things that Ysbaddaden wanted. Arthur himself fought with the Black Witch and gathered a bowlful of her blood. Cai snatched the sword of the mighty giant Wrnach. It was the only sword in the world that could kill the evil boar, Twrch Trwyth.

Twrch Trwyth carried a comb and scissors between his ears. They were the only comb and scissors strong enough to trim Ysbaddaden's hair.

But the boar was fierce and crafty. The knights chased him from Wales to Ireland and back again — and still they could not catch him.

They went to the Owl of Cwm Cawlwyd to ask for help.

'When I was born,' the owl said, 'this valley was full of trees. In time the trees all died and two more forests have since grown in their place. Though I'm so very very old and wise, I cannot help you catch the boar. He's much too cunning. Still I wish you luck.'

After a long hard chase the knights trapped Twrch Trwyth at last beside the sea in Cornwall. Though he struggled savagely, they snatched the comb and scissors from his head. Then the boar dived into the waves and was never seen again.

While the other knights lay sleeping, Gwythyr went for a walk on the hillside. There he heard a pitiful squeaking sound. It came from an ant-hill.

'The hill is on fire!' said Gwythyr. 'Those ants will be burnt!'

He ran to help them.

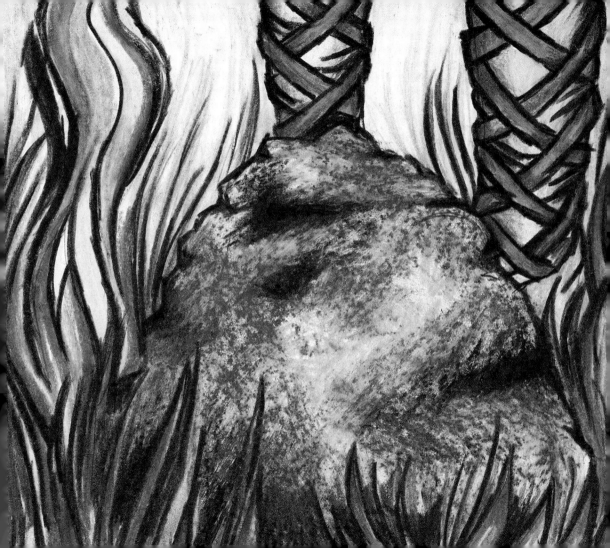

Gwythyr sliced through the ant-hill with his sword and lifted it out of harm's way.

An ant crawled onto his hand.

'Thank you,' said the ant in a thin little voice. 'You have saved our lives. Small as we are, we'd like to help you. Is there anything we can do?'

'Yes!' said Gwythyr.

He remembered the last of Ysbaddaden's tasks.

'Will you help me gather all the flax seed in Ysbaddaden's field before the sun goes down?' he asked.

'Of course,' said the ant. 'Put down some bowls and we'll fill them for you.'

The ants scurried over the field and plucked the flax seed from the ground.

'We must gather every single one,' Gwythyr said. 'The giant will count them.'

As the sun dipped down behind the hill, a lame ant hobbled up to him. On the ant's back was the very last seed.

Now at last Culhwch could return to the giant's castle.

He waited while Ysbaddaden's beard was shaved.

'I have done all you asked me,' Culhwch said. 'Now may I marry Olwen?'

'Huh! I suppose so,' the giant said sourly. 'But you wouldn't have done it on your own. It was Arthur who helped you.'

Those were the last words the giant spoke. His head was cut off by a young man whose brothers he had killed.

That very evening Culhwch and Olwen were married. After the wedding they were so happy they danced and feasted with King Arthur's knights for a month and a day.

A little help with pronunciation

(NOTE: § represents the sound 'ch' as in the Scottish word 'loch'
Ω is the Welsh 'll' (position the tongue to say 'l', then breathe out), as in 'Llanelli'
rr is the Welsh 'r' (always trilled, as in Scots/Spanish)
Bold print indicates stress

Culhwch — **Kill**-hoo§
Olwen — **Ol**-wenn
Ysbaddaden — Us-bah-**tha**-den (soft 'th' as in 'that')
Twrch Trwyth — Too-rr§ **Tru**ith (hard 'th' as in 'thin')
Arthur — **Arr**-thirr ('thirr' as in 'thin' but with 'rr' instead of 'n')
Cai — Kye
Bedwyr — **Bed**-wirr ('wirr' rhymes with 'thirr' in 'Arthur')
Gwythyr — **Gwi**thirr (as for 'Arthur')
Gwion — **Gwee**-on
Gwrhyr — **Goo-rr**-hirr ('goo' is short: 'hirr' rhymes with 'thirr' in 'Arthur')
Sgilti — **Skeel**ty (short 'ee')
Wrnach — **Oo**-rrna§ (short 'oo')
Cwm Cawlwyd — Kum (as in 'kum-ba-ya') **Cow**-luid